This book belongs to
Emersyn Lee

Written by Elanor Best.
Illustrated by Stuart Lynch.

CLUMP

THE LUMP OF COAL

WRITTEN BY ELANOR BEST

ILLUSTRATED BY STUART LYNCH

make
believe
ideas

CLUMP

I'm a GIFT for **naughty** KIDS each year, on

CHRISTMAS DAY.

But WHY **give** me to **that** lot when they all THROW ME **away?**

Not **EVERYBODY** knows this:

I'm not just a **fossil fuel.**

When you get to **know me,**

I'm **REALLY** kind of **cool!**

You can **USE ME** as a **crayon**

to create the **darkest splat.**

I make a **smoky,** SOOTY trail—
what **crayon** can do that?

Dear Santa,
for Christmas,
I would like
some new
crayons.
COAL

I can ALSO be a **building block** that's STACKED UP to the **sky.**

The OTHER toys seem **really** SMALL when I am WAY UP **high**.

I can EVEN be a **snowball** (that's just the WAY I ROLL).

But DON'T **throw** me at **children** . . .

In fact, I am so **VERY cool**,
there is a case to MAKE
for putting me in EVERY
bit of **Christmas**.
(<u>NOT</u> THE **CAKE!**)

FLOUR

I can be a PAPER CHAIN . . .

. . . or HANG upon the **tree.**

And I'd make a **stunning** ANGEL,

come on,

SANTA,

can't you **see?**

I don't **BELONG** in **Christmas** even though I **TRIED** my **best.**

"Wait a moment,
little Clump!
It's me who got it wrong.
As Santa,
it's my job to get you
somewhere you belong.
Will you let me fix this,
and jump on board
my sleigh?
There's somewhere
I would like to go . . .

"...although it's far away."

"Let me introduce
you, Clump,
to friendly Mr. Frost:
a snowman who has told me
about something that he lost . . ."

It's true!
It might sound silly,
but the stores are too remote
and I feel incomplete without
three buttons on my coat.

And, Clump, you won't believe it
but here's the funny twist:

every year,
a lump of coal
has been TOP of my list!

Welcome to **THE COAT!**

FINALLY, it seems I've found a **Christmas** I FIT IN.

And **BEST** of all, I've found new FRIENDS.

Now let the FUN begin . . .

I've LEARNED that I am **different,** NOTHING like a **Christmas** toy.

My DIFFERENCE makes me **special,** and BRINGS others so much **joy.**

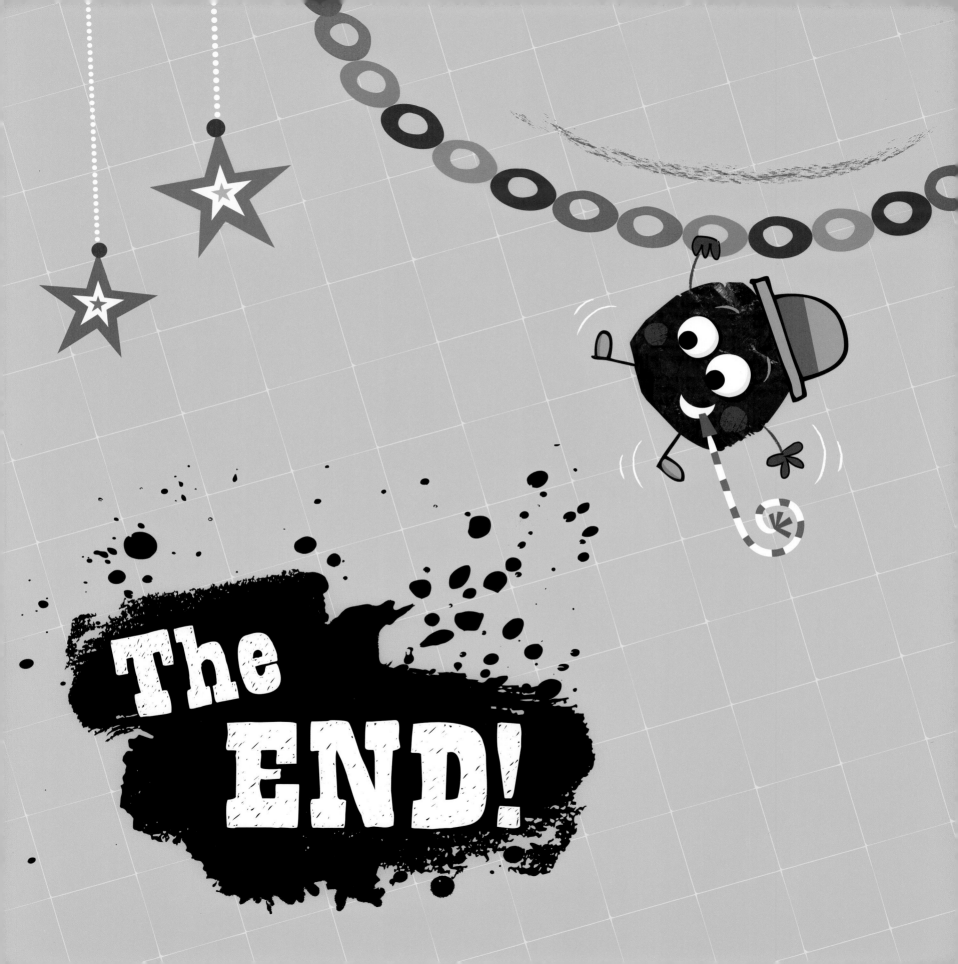

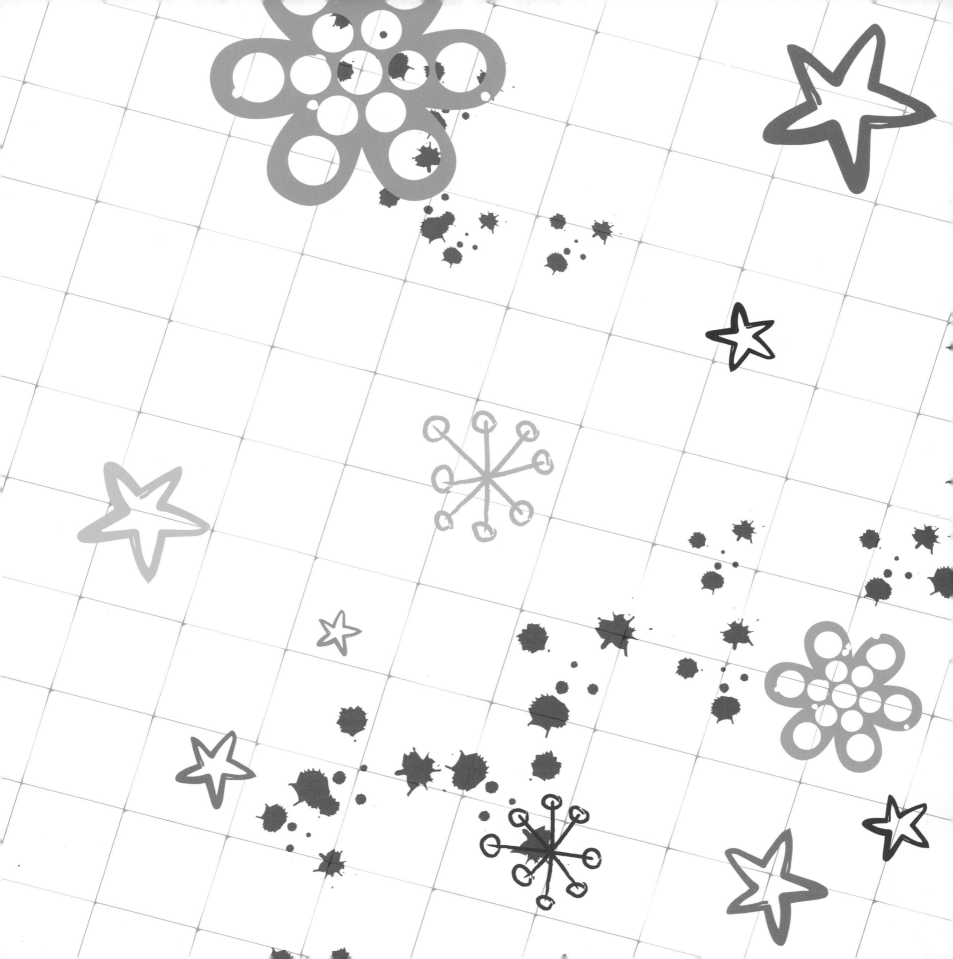